BEFORE I LET YOU GO

A NOVELLA

KIMBERLY BROWN

B. LOVE PUBLICATIONS

I REALLY DIDN'T WANT to go on this date, but I had promised my girl that I would try to get out and socialize. She had gone through a lot of trouble, that I didn't ask for, by the way, to set this whole thing up. Melissa had not so coincidently introduced me to Chad at her office last week. I had stopped by for our weekly lunch date, and he just so happened to be there "picking up some paperwork." When I walked in, a sly smile played across her face as she pointed and mouthed, *"That's him!"* I rolled my eyes when I turned around to close the door.

Melissa had been telling me for weeks that she had someone she wanted me to meet. She had even gone as far as sending me screenshots of his Facebook and Instagram pages. Chad was twenty-eight and had no children, his own place, car, and he was a professional. He wasn't bad on the eyes, either. In his toffee-colored skin, he stood about six feet even, with brown eyes and thick lips. He had a slim but muscular build. His hair was cut low and wavy. He was a handsome man, so I could see why she thought I would like him. That day he was dressed in maroon pants with a short-sleeve, black, polo style shirt that was tucked in. It showed off his muscular physique. His feet were housed by an expensive looking pair of black loafers.

"Rhyon!" Melissa exclaimed. "I was just talking about you!"

"Oh, I bet you were," I said sarcastically.

"Rhyon, this is Chad Michaels. Chad, this is my best friend since I was five years old, Rhyon Capers."

"Nice to meet you. Melissa showed me pictures, but they do absolutely no justice to this beauty in person."

I smiled. So he was a smooth talker.

"Why, thank you," I said as I set my bag down. I put our food on Melissa's desk.

"Let me get that for you," Chad said, pulling my chair out.

"How chivalrous of you."

"Well, my mama raised a gentleman."

"Are you close to your mother?" I asked trying to gauge whether he was a mama's boy. I didn't have time for that shit.

"We were. She passed away two years ago from breast cancer."

"Aww, I'm sorry to hear that."

"It's fine. We have some great memories, so her life was not in vain." He smiled at me. "I won't hold you guys up," he said. "Ms. Capers, do you mind if I get your number? I would love to get to know you."

I could see Melissa cheesing like a damn Cheshire cat in my peripheral. Chad seemed like a nice guy. It wasn't like I was seeing anyone anyway. A little conversation couldn't hurt.

"Sure." He handed me his phone and I saved my number in his contacts before handing it back to him.

"Thank you." He smiled. "I look forward to speaking with you. You ladies have a nice day."

"You too," I responded.

"Bye Chad!" Melissa said in a sing song voice. As soon as the door closed, she was on my ass. "So, what did you think of him?"

"From a five-minute conversation, Melissa?" I asked taking our food from the bag.

"First impressions. Hello!"

I rolled my eyes. "He's cute. Well mannered. Well dressed."

"You think you'd go on a date with him?"

"Is that what this was? Why are you trying to set me up, Melissa?"

"Because you need some dick, Rhyon," she answered, grabbing her plate of food.

"I don't have a problem getting dick. I'm just selective."

"When was the last time that you had a good fuck?"

"When was the last time that you had a good fuck?" I retorted, rolling my neck. I loved Melissa but I swear this ho was always in my damn business. I guess I couldn't be too mad because I was in hers too.

"Last night bitch. Now answer the question."

I was quiet. The last time I had my back blown the fuck out was about six months ago. I was messing around with this guy a few years younger than me. I wasn't looking for anything serious with him. I just needed to scratch an itch and this nigga looked and spoke like he was carrying a fucking baby arm in his pants. That young boy fucked the shit out of me. He was a nasty muthafucka, too. He sucked my toes, then ate my pussy and my ass before he fucked me into submission. I could barely walk for two days when he was done with me. That shit was grade A amazing. He had called me several times after that, but I ignored him. I couldn't be walking around here half handicapped after getting some dick. I had shit to do.

"As long as it is taking you to answer my question, I know that it has been a while," Melissa said, popping a piece of fried okra into her mouth.

"Whatever," I said, digging into my mac and cheese. "Chad doesn't even look like he would kill some pussy."

"Those are the ones that would surprise you! My secretary said she saw his print one day at the gym. Ol' boy is packing."

I rolled my eyes. "Melissa, I didn't come here to get set up. I came for our weekly lunch and gossip session. Spill me some tea, bitch!"

That's how it all started. Chad had called me that night and we talked on the phone for about two hours getting to know each other. He could actually hold an engaging conversation. He was smart and funny, funny not being something that I initially took him for. This carried on for about a week before he finally asked to take me to dinner. Melissa was excited. I'm sure her ass would be feeding him information about what I liked so that everything went smoothly.

As I sat at my vanity doing my makeup, I got an uneasy feeling in my stomach. I was nervous and that threatened to set off my anxiety. Something was bound to happen tonight. I didn't know what it was, but it had me on edge. I took a deep breath, popped one of my meds and tried to pump myself up for this date by turning on my ratchet playlist. Sometimes I just had to twerk that shit out. Chad rang my doorbell about six-thirty. I looked myself over once more then headed to the door. When I opened it, he stood there with a bouquet of poppies, my favorite flower, and a smile.

"Good evening, Rhyon," he said looking me over.

"Hey Chad."

"My God, you are breathtaking," he said kissing my cheek.

I had chosen a red off the shoulder dress with a ruffled top. Red was my signature color. I just loved the way it complimented my mocha skin tone. My dress was form fitting and stopped right above my knees. This baby hugged my size sixteen frame like a glove. My ass looked great in it. On my feet were a pair of gold pumps, making my five-foot six-inch frame appear at least three to four inches taller. I had pulled my braids up into a bun and simple gold jewelry accented my attire, along with a gold clutch.

"Thank you." I smiled. "You look very dapper yourself."

He was dressed in a black pants suit with a white, long-sleeve, button up covered with a black vest and wore black dress shoes. He looked very handsome.

"Thank you. These are for you." He handed me the flowers.

"These are my favorite," I said smelling them.

"A little birdie told me that." He smiled.

"Give me a second to put these in some water and I'll be ready." I turned and went into the kitchen and filled my empty vase with water. After putting the flowers in, I made sure everything I needed was in my clutch and joined him at the door.

"I'm all yours," I said.

"I like the sound of that," he said, offering me his arm.

I slid my arm through his and let him lead me to his car after locking my door. He must have been making bank at work because the car he drove was expensive. We settled in the car and we were on our way. He took me to this fancy upscale restaurant in the city called *Captain's Grill*. I knew this shit was about to be expensive too. I hoped that he wasn't trying to impress me by throwing his money around. That shit was a turn off. I made my own shit. To me, a man with money was a bonus, not a come up.

He got out of the car and rounded my side to open my door. Again, he offered me his arm as we headed inside. The hostess led us to a cozy secluded area that was dimly lit with soft candles. I slid into the booth and he slid in next to me. The hostess handed us the menus and told us that our server would be with us shortly.

"You look beautiful tonight, Rhyon," he said, covering my hand with his.

"Thank you," I said, offering a smile. "So, do you come here often?"

"From time to time. I like the atmosphere. Very chill, very relaxed. The perfect place to further get to know someone."

"How long have you been single, Chad?"

"Two years."

"That's a while. No entanglements?"

"If you are asking if I have had sex in those two years, I have. I still have needs as I'm sure you do as well."

"Touché."

The rest of the evening went decent. The food was amazing, the server was attentive, and Chad was pleasant. He kept me laughing the whole time. He really was a nice guy. Now I wasn't sure that I could see myself dating him seriously, but we could always be friends. When it came time for the check to come, he reached for his wallet but was stopped by our waitress.

"Oh no need, Mr. Michaels," she said. "The bill is taken care of."

"Come again?"

"A certain gentleman covered your table's tab." She smiled and pointed across the restaurant.

We looked around and my heart damn near jumped out of my chest when my eyes landed on *him*. I hadn't seen or heard from this man in over four years. *Emerald Hampton*. The man who had stolen my heart when we were kids. He was my first everything. My first crush. My first date, my first love. This was the man who took my virginity. He was also the reason that I had been single for almost the last five years. Emerald and I had known each other since elementary school. We were friends up until we started dating in high school, our sophomore year. We were together for six years. He had seen me through so many of the curveballs life threw at me. I never expected him to be my biggest one.

Emerald was a singer. And a damn good one I might add. He got his big break a year before we broke up, and it ultimately led to our demise. He wanted me to give up everything and move across the country. I was just finishing up undergrad and passed my bar exam. At the time I had just landed my job as a criminal defense attorney at one of the most prominent law offices in the state, courtesy of my professor. Not only that, but I had also been accepted into my graduate program. He knew how hard I was working on my law career. It was something I had been dreaming about since we were kids.

I couldn't leave. He didn't understand that. He wanted to take care of me, and I wanted to make my own way in the world. I never wanted to ride his coattails. I didn't want to throw away all my hard work to follow behind a man, no matter how much I loved him. We tried the long-distance thing for a year, and it broke me.

I missed him. I needed him and he wasn't able to be there for me. Our visits and communication became few and far in between. And then they just seemed to come to a halt. He was out living his best life and I was at home missing him. One day I got up my nerve to tell him it was time for us to go our separate ways. I blocked his number and tried to move on with my life. And now my past was staring me right in the face.

"Isn't that GEM?" Chad referred to his stage name, as he squinted across the crowded dining area.

"Yea," I mumbled.

"That was dope of him." He waved Emerald over.

"Please don't call him over here. Shit!"

"What's the matter?" Chad asked.

"I need to be excused." Before I could make a beeline to the bathroom, Emerald approached our table with a smile.

"Good evening," he said in that voice that use to soak my panties every time he said my name.

"Hey man, thanks for covering our tab," Chad said. "You didn't have to do that."

"It was nothing," he said, his eyes never leaving mine. He was burning a fucking hole through the side of my face. "You not gon' speak to me, Rhyon?"

I sighed, finally looking up at him. He was still as fine as he had ever been. Emerald stood six-three with a slim, but muscular build. He had beautiful chocolate skin. His hair was cut around the sides, leaving a curly patch on the top. I used to love to run my fingers through that shit. His eyes were hazel and could easily pierce my fucking soul. Those lips...those juicy ass lips used to be all over my body marking their territory. I shuddered at the thought of his mouth being on my lips, whether it be the upper or lower ones.

"Hey Emerald," I said quietly.

"You two know each other?" Chad asked.

"We used to date," I mumbled.

"Seriously?"

"Yeah..."

"Oh, don't be modest, Rhyon," Emerald said sitting down, right next to me at our booth. "We dated for six years before this little lady broke my heart."

"Funny how I remember that differently," I said motioning for Chad to get out of the booth. "I'm on a date, Emerald. I'm going to the bathroom and when I get back, I expect you to be gone."

I quickly slid out of the booth and practically ran to the bathroom. I was almost hyperventilating. Emerald was the last person I expected to see tonight or at any time for that matter. He had been doing his thing all over the world for the last four years. What could he possibly be doing back home now? I took out my phone and called Melissa.

"Hello!" she sang.

"Melissa *he's* here."

"Well, you did agree to go out with him, Rhyon..."

"I'm not talking about Chad! I'm talking about muthafucking Emerald Hampton!"

"What!"

"He's at the restaurant! Melissa, he paid for our dinner. Chad was fucking star struck and waved him over to the table."

"Did he say anything to you?"

"You know he did."

"How's he looking?"

"Melissa!"

"Bitch I know you looked!"

"He looked so good Melissa," I whined. "Why did he have to be here? Chad and I were having a good time. I was enjoying myself. And here he comes fucking up my mental like only he can do. I was doing so good without him. I finally had him out of my system and here his ass is."

I started crying. Melissa was trying to comfort me, but it was no use. I could escape Emerald out in the world. I didn't have to see him. I could choose not to listen to his music or watch him in videos, concerts or interviews. I couldn't escape him here. Here, he was home. He was regular old Emerald Hampton.

There was a knock on the door that forced me back to reality.

"I gotta go, Melissa." I sniffed.

"Call me when you get home."

"Okay."

I ended the call and tried to fix my makeup and compose myself. When I opened the door, this muthafucka was standing there looking at me with a smile on his face.

"Move," I said.

"Come on, Rhyon...don't be like that with me baby."

"I am not your baby, Emerald."

"You'll always be my baby." He reached out and cupped my face and my body froze. I could feel the goosebumps on my skin. My breathing became labored.

"See how your body is responding to me?" he said seductively, as he clasped his hand around the back of my neck. That shit always made me hot.

"Did you miss me, Rhyon?"

"No..." I whispered as his lips kissed my cheek.

"You sure about that baby?" He wrapped an arm around my waist and pulled me into his chest. "Cause I missed you..."

I felt his lips on my collar bone.

"You look beautiful. And you smell good," he whispered rubbing his nose against my neck. At this point I don't think I was breathing at all. "How you gon do me like that, Rhyon?" he asked pulling back. He gently grabbed my neck and traced my bottom lip with his thumb. "You just broke a nigga heart."

I snapped back to reality.

"You wanted me to give up everything for you, Emerald..."

"No, I wanted to take care of you like I promised I would. None of this shit means anything if I don't have you baby."

"Well, it looks like you made it just fine without me," I said finding the strength to push him from me. "Can you let me get back to my date?"

"Ol' boy ain't even your type, Rhyon..."

"It's been four years, Emerald. You don't know me anymore."

"Oh, I know you baby. I know you like the back of my hand. It's cool though. I'll let you ride this one out. Let him enjoy your presence tonight. Just remember one thing."

"And what would that be?" I asked throwing up my hands.

He pushed me up against the wall and in a split second his lips were on mine. I wanted to protest. I wanted to push him from me. But I felt myself getting hot. When he slipped his tongue in my mouth and gripped my ass, a low moan escaped my throat.

He finally pulled away, wiping the corners of my mouth.

"I still love you, Rhyon. I gave you time to do what you needed to do for you. But you need to know that you are mine still. I came back for you. And I'm not leaving until I have you."

He left me standing there in my feelings with my mouth open and my panties soaking wet. Damn him! I got myself together and went back to the table. Chad looked concerned.

"I thought I'd have to come get you," he said. "Are you okay, Rhyon?"

"I'm fine, Chad."

"Are you sure? You look upset."

"Emerald and I have a long history. I've known him since I was in elementary school. We started dating our sophomore year in high school and we were together throughout college."

"Wow. I imagine it's hard seeing him. You looked like you wanted to jump out of your skin."

"I certainly felt like it. We didn't end on the best of terms. Seeing him here tonight, I don't know." I looked up at him. "I'm sorry if I ruined our date, Chad."

"Nonsense. You were perfect. But I get the feeling this may be our first and last date."

"I'm sorry..." I said holding my head down.

"Don't be. I see it between you two. Even if you can't admit it, you still feel something for him, Rhyon. I won't try to stand in the way or convince you or myself otherwise."

I sighed. "You're a great person Chad. I know you'll find someone who can give you what you deserve."

"We can always be friends."

"I'd like that. I could always use another friend."

"I guess we'll have to break the news to Melissa." He chuckled.

"Trust me, she'll be setting you up again in no time." I smiled lightly.

"Well, she has great taste, I'll give her that. You're a beautiful woman, Rhyon." He kissed my cheek. Then he grinned at me. "At least I can say Emerald Hampton stole my woman. That's a little bragging right."

I giggled. "You're silly. Come on. We can go back to my place and watch some movies."

"I'm down for that." He slid out of the booth and helped me to my feet. After offering me his arm, we headed out.

 merald

GODDAMN, Rhyon was looking good as a muthafucka! The last four years had been good to her. Her body in that dress had my dick screaming, *"Lawd, have mercy on my soul!"* She had gained a little weight over the years but that shit filled her out in all the right places. That ass! It took more than everything in me not to take her in the bathroom and fuck the shit out of her. That woman always had the ability to entice all five of my senses.

Just looking at her sent sensations through my body. Her voice soothed my soul. I loved running my hands all over her supple, velvet skin. Her natural scent made my mouth water. And when I feasted on the sweet nectar from the honey pot between her legs, my taste buds were never more satisfied. Rhyon Capers was it for me. She always had been. I was devastated when she broke up with me, but I understood why. I couldn't be physically present, and I dropped the ball when it came to being there emotionally after I moved away. My career was just taking off, so I was grinding all day every day. Studio time. Rehearsals. Booking shows. My intent was never to leave her behind. I wanted her with me.

I wanted to take care of her and give her the world. But I knew she needed to establish her independence. That's why I told myself that I would wait for her to finish school before I asked her to move with me across the country again. Somewhere along the line, I lost sight of that while trying to make a name for myself. When she broke up with me, I threw myself into my work to prove to her that it would all pay off. Now I was selling out concerts and arenas. My album sales were skyrocketing, and I had more money in the bank than I knew what to do with. The only thing missing was sharing it with the woman I had loved since my first day at Calvin Oaks Elementary School.

The cute little chocolate doll with pigtails had turned into a beautiful goddess and I was ready to claim her. She was still mine. And I was going to show her that. When I pulled up to my parents' house, I had to smile. With all the money I made, I offered to buy them a new home. They adamantly declined telling me my money would be better spent elsewhere. They loved the home they had been sharing for the last thirty years. They said it held too many memories to ever part from. I understood that. Hell, I had hella memories in that house. I sang my first note there. I used to put on concerts for my aunties and family members in our living room. My mama loved to show me off.

"Go on and sing that lil' song baby!" she would always tell me. She was my biggest supporter. She was also my manager until my career took off. She refused to let anybody dupe me into a deal that wouldn't benefit me. "Know your worth and make them pay you for it." She always told me that. When I got my big break, she found me a manager with the same mindset, and we have been making money together ever since.

I got out of my rental with flowers in hand for my mother and a box of Cuban cigars for my pops. They had no idea that I was home. I had gotten in early yesterday evening and checked into my hotel. I had my bags in the car, as I was spending the remainder of my time with them. I walked up the driveway to the front porch and rang the doorbell.

"Just a minute!" my mother called.

I stood there with a huge smile plastered to my face. I hadn't been home at all in the four years I had been chasing this music shit. When my mother opened the door, she screamed and jumped in my arms.

"My baby! Oh, I'm so happy to see you!"

"Hey ma," I said squeezing her tightly. I could feel her tears on my shirt. She cupped my face and kissed my cheeks several times before hugging me again. My father came running around the corner.

"What are you screaming about woman?" he asked before he saw me.

"Hey pop," I said stepping in.

"Emerald Hampton!" he said smiling wide. He pulled me in for an embrace. "My boy!"

My mother came up behind me and they sandwiched me in. I felt so much love at that moment. I didn't realize how much I missed them. Calls and video chats were nice but being able to touch them, being home, that shit hit different.

"Let me get a look at you!" my mom said holding me away from her. I did a smooth turn for her and posed.

"You look good baby! Even more handsome than I remember!" she kissed my cheek again. "I'm so happy your home, Em."

"It's good to be home, Ma. I see y'all missed me!"

"Always, son. What are you doing here?"

"I decided to take a break from the music for a lil' bit. I been at this nonstop for the last four years. I'm tired. I've done more than I set out to do. I'm ready to share it with the one person who was supposed to be by my side the whole ride."

They smiled. "Well, it's about damn time," my father said.

I chuckled. "I've let her do everything she set out to do. It's time to claim her."

"Well, you better pull out all the stops," my mother said. "You know I talk to her every week. We even have lunch sometimes and she has long since stopped asking about you, Emerald. I know she holds a lot of emotions attached to your breakup that she hasn't dealt with. It was like she pushed you out of her mind."

"Well, I have a plan to get her back, Ma. She might be able to push me to the back of her mind, but she can never push me out of her heart."

"Well, she'll be in for a surprise when she sees you."

"I saw her last night."

"Oh? Where?"

"*Captain's Grill,* you know that fancy restaurant in the city?"

"The one with all those high ass prices for mediocre food?"

"The food is good." I chuckled. "Everybody ain't blessed by the hand of God to cook like you, Mama."

"I know that's right! Wait a minute! You been here since last night and we are just seeing you!" My mother slapped my arm.

"You got me for a whole day!" I laughed. "Actually, you'll have me while I'm here. That is if my bedroom is still available."

"You always have a room in this house, Emerald," my mother said. "So, what was her reaction to seeing you?"

"Well after I paid for her and her date's dinner..."

"Emerald, I know you didn't!" my mother exclaimed.

"I had to get her attention, Ma!"

"I know you embarrassed that man!"

"Actually, he called me over to say thank you."

"What about Rhyon?"

"In not so many words, she told me to get lost."

"Damn," Pops said shaking his head.

"I wasn't accepting that. So, when she excused herself to the bathroom, I followed her..."

My mother gave me a look.

"Calm down, Ma, I just waited on her to come out. She doesn't know it, but I heard her conversation with Melissa. She was telling her how good I looked and then she started crying. That broke my heart all over again."

"Did she ever talk to you?"

"Nooooot in so many words, but she definitely responded to my words and actions."

"Emerald!" My mother turned red.

"Not like that, Ma!" I laughed. "Well maybe a little like that. There was a little touching...a little kissing. Not quite PG-13 but not quite Rated R."

"Don't seduce her, Emerald," she said seriously. "If you love her like I know you do, let her come to you naturally. I know she still loves you. I feel that in my spirit. Just give her time to ease into this. There are conversations that y'all need to have."

"I know, Ma. I'm sure I accomplished one thing though."

"What?"

"She definitely won't be able to push me to the back of her mind again."

"Well, I have to see this," Pops said. "We tend to under-estimate a woman's ability to be through with our ass."

"I got this, Pop. I'm not leaving until I claim my woman."

I meant that shit in every sense of the words. Rhyon could play hard but I could play harder. I was prepared to pull out all the stops this time around. I let her get away once and she was never getting away again.

I HAD a ball with my parents yesterday. We went to visit family that I hadn't seen or spoken to while I was away. It felt good to be home. Back to my old stomping grounds. I had made a few stops to some of my favorite places in town, including my old high school. The principal was so happy to see me that she had me visit one of the music classes and visit the kids in the cafeteria. I signed autographs and took pictures with damn near everyone. Before I left, I wrote her a check for twenty-five thousand dollars to donate to their music program. That place had really jumpstarted my career. I wanted to keep that hope alive for other students.

My last stop of the day was to Rhyon's parents' house. I used to practically live at this place. It was my home away from home. Her parents loved me, especially her mother. When I pulled up in the yard, her mom was outside getting groceries out of the car. Mr. Capers had just come out to help her. When they saw my car pull up behind theirs, they stopped and waited to see who would step out.

"Can I stay for dinner?" I asked with a smile.

"Emerald!" her mother screamed. She put her bags down and scooped me up in a hug so tight I think my feet left the ground. "It's so good to see you baby!" She kissed my cheek.

"It's good to see you too, Ma. How are you, Mr. Capers?" I asked, dapping, then embracing him.

"I'm alive and well. Good to have you home, son. You been away how long now?"

"Four years."

"That's a long time. I see life has been treating you well. Congratulations on all of your success."

"Thank you. You can actually thank your daughter for that. She was the inspiration behind a lot of my music," I confessed.

"Oh, we know that. You don't sing with that much soul and emotion without feeling it first-hand."

"You listen to my music, Mr. Capers?"

"Every song, every album. We are some of your biggest fans. I proudly tell people I use to feed that boy!"

I laughed. "Yea, you never let me go hungry."

"Boy you almost ate me out of house and home."

"But you never turned me away. I'll never forget that."

"Of course not. You were family. You're *still* family."

"That means more to me than you know." I smiled. "Let me get this for you," I said grabbing a hand full of grocery bags. Mr. Capers grabbed the rest while his wife got her keys and purse. We went inside and I sat at the kitchen island talking to them while they put their items up. We had been talking a good ten minutes when Mrs. Capers asked the looming question.

"Does Rhyon know you're back?"

"Yes ma'am...she wasn't happy to see me at first, but I plan to change her mind."

"You know Rhyon can be a little set in her ways."

"Just like her mama." Mr. Capers chuckled.

"And her big head ass daddy." His wife giggled mushing his head. He grabbed her hand and kissed it.

"I know," I said. "I'm gonna work on that while I'm here."

"How long are you in town for?"

"As long as it takes."

"Takes to what?" Mrs. Capers asked.

"To get his woman back," Mr. Capers answered for me with a wink. "Pay attention, Corrina."

"Oh, hush up, Raymond...you really came back for her, Emerald?"

"Yes ma'am. I love that woman the same as I ever did. I'm hoping she'll give me a chance to love the parts of her that developed in my absence."

"I know what that means," Mr. Capers joked.

"No not like that." I laughed.

"I know, I know."

"But seriously, I'm ready to meet this version of her. Learn her. Love her and cherish her. There will never be another woman for me other than your daughter."

They looked at each other and smiled.

"Maybe we'll get a grandbaby out of this," Mrs. Capers whispered, giggling.

"Whoa wait!" I laughed. "I have to get her to actually take me seriously first."

"Well, you can start today. She's on her way over here."

"Really?"

"Yep. Should be pulling up any minute."

My face felt hot all of a sudden. I wasn't expecting to see her again so soon. At least not before I could set my plans in motion.

"You okay, Emerald?" Mrs. Capers asked noticing my sudden silence. "You're sweating baby."

"Them nerves got his ass," Mr. Capers laughed loudly. "How do you have a plan, but you sweat the minute you know she's about to be in your presence?"

"I'm human!" I defended.

"No worries. Nerves just mean you want it bad enough." He slapped my shoulder. "Forget about whatever plan you have concocted in your head and just go with it. Take a deep breath."

They went back to cleaning up the mess from the grocery bags as I sat there anticipating Rhyon's arrival. About ten minutes had passed before I heard the front door opening.

"Hey who's car is that in the driveway..." She came walking into the kitchen but stopped as soon as she saw me. My eyes had a mind of their own as they traveled her body from head to toe. She was dressed in a black, suspender short set with a white, short-sleeve crop-top and black sandals. Her white polish was begging me to suck her toes.

She rolled her eyes.

"Hey, Rhyon." I smiled standing.

"Emerald. What are the chances of you being here, at *my* parents' house?" She cocked her head to the side and crossed her arms.

"You know this was like my second home."

"Well, that was a long time ago."

"Rhyon!" her mother scolded. "Emerald is always welcome here. Apologize."

"Mommy..."

"Apologize."

She sighed. "I'm sorry, Emerald."

She sounded like a child.

"It's okay. I know that's just your defense mechanisms at work."

"Well, I have a lot to be defensive about..."

"Rhyon," her mother warned.

"Ma. I don't know what you want me to do. I'm sure Emerald didn't expect me to welcome him back with open arms. A heads up would have been nice. At least I could have chosen if I wanted to see him yet. This is the second time in forty-eight hours he's shown up in my space and I've just had to deal with it. That's not fair. I feel like I'm being forced, and I don't like that."

She turned and walked back out the door. I followed behind her. She was sitting on the front porch with her head in her hands. I took a seat beside her. We sat there in silence for about five minutes.

"I'm sorry, baby," I said finally.

She glared at me.

"I mean I'm sorry, Rhyon. It was a coincidence that we ended up at the same spot for dinner the other night. Although I probably could have done better with making my presence known. I didn't show up with ill intent today. I didn't even know you were coming until I got here. You know I love your parents. I just wanted to see them. I didn't mean to piss you off."

"What do you want from me, Emerald?" she asked standing up. "Huh? What are you hoping to accomplish?"

"I told you," I said standing to my feet and stepping closer to her. "I came back for you, Rhyon."

"What makes you think I want you back?"

"Because you know you still love me, too," I said reaching out and cupping her face. She shivered under my touch. "You see that?" I asked bringing attention to it. "Your body says everything you won't. That was evident at dinner. Look me in my eyes and tell me you don't love me."

She looked at me, tears threatening her eyes.

"That isn't enough, Emerald."

"I have so much more to give to you, Rhyon. You were always meant to be mine."

I kissed her softly on the lips and pulled her into my arms. She hesitantly wrapped her arms around my waist and held me tight.

"I just want you to let me in, Rhyon. I know we have a lot to talk about before you let me pursue you. Why don't you let me come over tonight? We can start there. I promise I'll be on my best behavior."

She pulled away from me, crossing her arms. "I don't know."

"Please baby. My spirit is craving your presence, Rhyon." I kissed her lips again and this time she kissed me back. "I love you baby...I need you," I whispered against her mouth. I kissed her deeper this time, keeping my arms at her waist. Her lips parted and welcomed my tongue. Her arms came around my neck, caressing the back of my head. A moan escaped her throat.

"Can I see you, Rhyon?" I asked again.

"Yes." She forced herself away from me. "Come on," she said taking my hand. We headed back inside the house. Her parents were seated in the living room. They looked up at us when we sat next to each other on the couch. Then they looked at each other and smiled but didn't say anything about it.

"So, I'm sure your parents were happy to see you, Emerald," Mrs. Capers said.

"Yes ma'am. Mama screamed so loud she almost burst my ear drums. Then she started crying. It definitely made me regret not coming home sooner." I looked down for a moment, thinking about all the time I missed out on with spending with them. I had been so busy the last couple of years, I barely had time for myself let alone anyone else. I was going to make the most of this vacation.

"They really missed you."

"I missed them too. I didn't realize how much until I came back. I might have to kidnap them and take them with me. I've been trying to get them to come on tour with me for years now. They have been to a few shows, but they say they can't take all the noise. They have watched every performance though."

"Really?"

"Every single one," I smiled. "I always have my assistant live stream it so they could see."

"You plan on releasing anything new?" Mr. Capers asked.

"I might do a little writing while I'm here if I find some inspiration." I looked over at Rhyon who was playing with her nails. She must have sensed me and looked up.

"How long are you going to be here?" she asked.

"That depends."

"On?"

"Several things. I guess we'll just have to see how my visit goes. I've cleared my schedule for a few weeks though."

She nodded, trying to hide the smile that threatened to appear on her beautiful face. I couldn't wait to spend time with her later.

hyon

I WAS nervous as shit about having Emerald in my house. I wanted so bad to stay mad at him. To shut him out. It was much easier when he was away. Now that he was here in the flesh, I couldn't seem to hold on to the anger I felt for him. Emerald had a way of getting under my skin. He knew he was my weakness. Whenever he touched me, I forgot all about being upset. My body still craved him after all these years. It was fucking crazy.

"I don't know what I'm getting into, Melissa," I said as I cleaned up. I had called her over to talk my nerves down, but of course this bitch was no help.

"Just go with it, Rhyon," she said flinging herself across my bed. "It's not like you aren't familiar with that man."

"I'm familiar with the Emerald we grew up with. I don't know what all has changed in four years. He could be someone I don't even like."

"Or he could be the same Emerald you have loved since we were fifteen. I don't know why you are acting like you don't want to see him. Look at how you're running around here trying to make sure everything is perfect. Like you want to make a good impression."

"I don't...I don't know what you're talking about," I said.

"Bullshit. Just make sure you shower and trim that coochie hair bitch."

"Fuck you, Melissa."

"That's exactly what is going to happen when Emerald gets here."

"No, it's not!" I yelled, throwing my slipper at her.

"Girl please. You know you miss the dick. All the stories you told me about him having you practically climbing the damn walls. Your pussy is gonna pounce on him the minute he says the right thing."

"I don't know why I called your ass over here."

"Cause you love me and I'm the voice of reason when you're being anal. What time is he coming over?"

"About eight. He said he was having dinner with his parents."

"Well I'll leave when he shows up. I gotta dig in his ass about not even reaching out to me since his black ass been here. Like damn. I know you are top priority but the nigga was my friend too."

"I'm sure he'll be happy to see you too."

Melissa got up from my bed and went into my closet. "So what are you going to wear?"

"I don't know. Something comfortable."

"With easy access!"

"Melissa!"

She laughed loudly. "I'm playing girl. You should see your face."

"I can't with you," I said tossing my head back.

I continued to clean while Melissa cracked jokes and made light of just how bad my nerves were right now. When I was done I took a shower, moisturized my skin, then found something to wear. I settled on a pair of leggings that did wonders for my thighs and ass and a crop top that showed off the large tattoo on my side. I decided to forego any makeup, only using a little lip gloss. I let my braids hang free. I looked myself over in the mirror as Melissa sat on my bed watching with a smirk.

"What?" I asked with my hands on my hips.

"Nothing, nothing..." she smiled.

"Say it."

"Your ass looks amazing in that shit. Ain't no way he's gonna keep his hands off of you...Or maybe you don't want him to."

"Go to hell Melissa," I laughed.

We headed into the kitchen and I poured us up a shot. I needed something to take the edge off. Emerald would be here in a few minutes. We sat there talking for a bit, me sitting on the kitchen island and her on the bar stool. When the doorbell rang, I froze.

"Well, are you going to answer?" Melissa giggled.

"I'm going, I'm going!" I hopped down off of the island and headed to the door. My hand lingered on the knob for a second, as I took a deep breath, then I opened it. Emerald stood there with a bottle of my favorite wine and a smile. He was dressed in a yellow muscle t-shirt, a pair of black shorts and crisp, white sneakers. He looked like a fucking snack.

"Hey Rhyon," came his baritone voice. My pussy was throbbing looking at him.

"Hey Emerald." I smiled. He pulled me into a warm embrace, and I damn near melted when I smelled him. I just wanted to lick him. A low moan escaped my throat and he chuckled.

"What was that?" he asked.

"You smell good." I giggled. I had to stop doing that shit. I was annoying my damn self. He made me feel like we were teenagers all over again.

"Well, I'm glad you like it."

I stepped aside and let him in. The minute I closed the door Melissa was on his ass.

"Now I know your black ass didn't come home and leave me hanging nigga," she said playfully punching him.

"I could never forget your goofy ass Melissa." He laughed, pulling her in for a hug. "I missed your sense of humor."

"Is that why you haven't hit me up in how long?"

"You got me," he said holding his hands up. "I've been a shitty friend."

"You can always make it up to me by introducing me to one of your fine ass industry friends."

"You don't want them niggas, Melissa. They ain't shit. I'd hate to have to fuck one of them up for trying to fuck you over."

"When did you become a roughneck?" she laughed. "I can take care of myself, Emerald."

"That might be so, but you are also my friend. I wouldn't set you up for the okey doke."

She rolled her eyes and smiled. She knew as well as I did, that she appreciated Emerald looking out for her. Melissa like to play hard, but she was a big ass baby.

"I'm gonna head out and give you two some privacy." She winked. "We need to do lunch soon. Don't make me hunt your ass down, Emerald."

"I got you." He chuckled. She hugged him goodbye and kissed his cheek. Then she grabbed her bag and came to hug me.

"I hope you get some tonight bitch," she whispered in my ear.

"Goodbye Melissa!" I said rolling my eyes. She waved me off and headed out the front door, leaving Emerald and I alone. I could feel his eyes on me as I stood nervously playing with my nails.

"Come here, Rhyon," he said sitting the bottle of wine down.

I looked up and slowly made my way over to him. He took my hands in his, gently caressing them with the pads of his thumbs.

"Thank you for spending time with me alone," he said.

I nodded, my voice caught in my throat.

"I want you to relax," he said moving to cup my face. "It's just me. You know me, Rhyon."

I took a deep breath and nodded. "I'm glad you're here, Emerald," I whispered.

He smiled. "Really now?"

"I've missed you," I said pulling away and going to sit on the couch.

He took a seat beside me. We sat in silence for a few seconds before I fully turned to him.

"When I left you, it broke my heart, Emerald. I understand you wanted to follow your dreams. I would never fault you for that. I just feel like after a while you left me behind. I was here trying to support my own dreams and yours and you just abandoned me. If you couldn't always be here physically you could have been there for me emotionally..."

I sat there for a moment. Contemplating the word vomit that had invaded my mouth. I was about to drop some shit on him that I had been keeping a secret for years.

"Emerald....I was pregnant."

His eyes widened. "What?"

"I was pregnant when you left. I was about six weeks along when I found out."

"What...I mean how.... I mean where..." He was flustered. "Why didn't you tell me?"

"I didn't want to stop you from taking your big break..."

"That was my child, Rhyon!" he yelled.

"I know. I didn't tell anyone."

"What did you do?"

I dropped my head.

"I had a miscarriage," I said quietly. "I was about twelve weeks. I had been having a bad feeling for a few days before it happened. Like something bad was coming. I was at home when I felt the cramping. I knew what was happening...it took everything in me not to scream and cry. I bore through that pain and drove myself to the hospital. By the time I got there I was covered in blood. It was over. They cleaned me out, gave me meds and in a few hours I went home."

I started to cry at the memory.

"Why didn't you tell me, Rhyon? I would have been there for you. I would have come home."

"I tried to tell you, Emerald! I called you. I told you I needed you. I showed you that. Maybe not verbally, but Emerald, I wasn't myself for weeks and you were so busy you didn't even notice! Everyone thought I was just upset and missing you, but I was dying inside. Dying! The man that I loved that I thought knew me inside out, didn't see the biggest change in me. I knew you, Emerald. I knew your feelings. Your moods. I could always sense when something was wrong or off with you because I was that in tuned with you. I thought you were the same with me. But you were so caught up in your career, you didn't care."

"That's not fair, Rhyon. I've always cared about you. How was I supposed to know something that deep if you didn't tell me? You didn't talk to me about it, Rhyon."

"When was I supposed to talk to you, Emerald? You started having your assistant answer your calls. When we did speak it was brief. I didn't see you for months at a time."

"That's not an excuse. You should have told me you were pregnant the moment you found out. I would have made it a priority!"

"It being me should have been priority enough!" I yelled. "I was your woman! And you pushed me to the side like I was nothing! For an entire year I dealt with being put on the back burner. You changed. You moved away and everything with us just went from sugar to shit."

"I wanted you to come with me. I wanted you right by my side."

"You know I couldn't leave. I had just started working and I was about to start my master's program."

"There were jobs and schools out there, Rhyon! You could have transferred!"

"Why? So I could move out there and still be alone? Away from my family, my friends, for you to be gone more than you were home? I could have stayed here for that and I did. I got that job because I worked hard to prove myself. I couldn't just give that up to follow you around."

"I was trying to make a better life for us. Not just for me. I wanted to marry you, Rhyon. I wanted to take care of you. Provide for you everything you deserved..."

"All I wanted was you! I didn't care about the money or the material things, Emerald! *You* were enough for me!"

We stared at each other in silence. The tension in the room was so thick you could slice it with a knife. I wiped my face and turned away from him. My miscarriage was something I swore I would take to my grave. It was a place of hurt and anger when being pregnant was supposed to be a happy occasion. I still had my ultrasound picture tucked away in the back of my closet in a box that held all my memories of Emerald. I told myself I would never tell him. It was a part of my life that I needed to let go of just like I had let him go. Only I hadn't let him go at all. I just buried him away in the back of my mind, much like I had buried away his memories. Now he was back in the flesh and everything I thought died a long time ago was resurfacing.

I felt him shift on the couch then I felt his presence next to me.

"Rhyon," he whispered.

I shook my head no and held up my hand as I fought back tears.

"Rhyon look at me," he said softly.

He turned my head to his, forcing me to look at him. "I'm sorry it seemed like I pushed you away baby. That was never my intention. You've always been it for me. I'm sorry I neglected you. I'm sorry that I wasn't there when you needed me. Not just with losing our child, but for every time you needed me over the last five years that I wasn't there. Even if we weren't together, I shouldn't have gone through life without maintaining a friendship or at least reaching out to you. You were more than my woman, Rhyon, you were my best friend. I've missed you so much."

He pulled me into his arms and held me.

"Please let me make it up to you. Allow me to show you that I can be everything you wanted and all that you need."

"I don't know, Emerald," I whispered. "I'm not the same person that you left when you moved away. I'm different now."

"Then allow me to get to know you again." He cupped my face. "I want to fall in love with every part of you, Rhyon."

He kissed me softly. I was confused. I had loved this man almost my entire life, first as a friend, then as a lover. But at this moment, I didn't trust him like I used to. I didn't trust him not to forget me again. How could I trust him with my heart? I pulled away from him.

"I need some time to think about this."

I stood and went into the kitchen to make myself another drink. A strong drink at that. The last three days had been mentally draining for me. My anxiety was through the roof. I felt like I was on edge. I needed to make an appointment to see my therapist soon. It had been a few weeks since my last visit, which was good compared to the times where I needed to see her on a weekly basis. I had been seeing Dr. Claytor since Emerald and I had broken up, another secret that I had kept from everyone. No one knew exactly how hard it was for me when he left. I didn't know how to live without him.

How do you go from seeing someone every day and sleeping next to them every night, to seeing them every couple of months to not seeing them at all? How do you deal with losing the person that was your peace and place of comfort? The person you grew with? Maybe it was unhealthy to have that type of attachment to someone. But I felt in my heart that Emerald was my soulmate. The demise of our relationship brought about anxieties in other areas of my life. At times it was overwhelming. That's when I went to see Dr. Claytor. The way that I was feeling right now, I would be making a visit to her ASAP.

Emerald followed me into the kitchen. He came up behind me as I stood at my island and wrapped his arms around my waist. I closed my eyes and leaned into him. He hummed softly in my ear as he kissed my neck. Then he started singing and rocking me back and forth. He hadn't sung to me in years. It used to be his way of calming my nerves whenever I felt overwhelmed. It worked back then. But right now all he was doing was making my ass horny. I turned around in his arms as he continued to sing and stared at him. I was trying to feel his words, but my pussy was trying to feel his dick.

Before I could stop myself, my hands traveled up his chest, to his neck. I traced the tattoo he had of my lips. I replaced the ink with my own lips. Never distracted from singing, Emerald ran his fingers through my braids and my lips made their way from his neck to his earlobe. My hands gripped the ends of his shirt as I slowly peeled it away from his body. He continued to sing as he stared as my eyes traveled his body for the new artwork he had accumulated. My fingers traced over his chest piece in awe.

His entire chest was a dedication to me. My name, my birthday, my zodiac sign, and things like my favorite flowers were imprinted in his skin. I looked up at him and he stopped singing.

"When did you get this?" I asked almost in a whisper.

"A few years ago. I got one and then just kept adding to it."

"Emerald, this is beautiful."

"I've carried you with me all these years, Rhyon," he said cupping my face. "I never forgot about you."

The moment that our lips collided, I knew that my world was about to change. Emerald lifted me into his arms and placed me on the countertop. He stood between my legs and pulled my shirt over my head. His lips went to my neck. He placed soft kisses on the tops of my breasts as he reached around to unhook my bra. When my titties were free, his lips latched on to my nipples. I felt shock waves radiating through me. His tongue circled my hardened buds and then he flicked it rapidly across it. A moan escaped my throat.

"Oooo, Em."

He pushed me onto my back on the counter as his hands went to remove my leggings and boy shorts. I laid before him completely naked and utterly vulnerable. Emerald lifted my feet and kissed my toes before taking the big one into his mouth. The eye contact he was giving me as he sucked my toes was so fucking erotic that I could barely breathe. He made his way up my body, kissing, sucking, and nibbling on the back of my legs as he did. I was so turned on that by the time he reached my pussy, I was liable to cum if he breathed on me too hard. He draped both of my legs across his shoulders and kissed the insides of my thighs. The moment he ran his tongue up my slit I thought that I would die. I let out and exasperated breath when the tip of his tongue graced my clit. He teased me with a sensual assault on my pearl. He ate my pussy in a slow fashion that would only make my orgasm that much more powerful.

"Emerald," I moaned grabbing my legs to hold them up allowing him full access to me. I felt his tongue slip into my canal. He used his thumb to play with my clit as he fucked me with his mouth. I knew my shit was wet enough to soak him. When his tongue replaced his thumb, his fingers replaced his tongue. He quickly found my g-spot and made it his mission to make me lose my mind.

"Oooo.... SHIT!" I cried out with pleasure. My left hand went to his hair to grip it as I propped myself up with my right arm so I could watch him. He ate my pussy like it was his last meal. He was threatening to push me over the edge and I was about to let him do it.

"Oh God! What are you doing to me!" I moaned as his eyes locked on mine. I came within seconds. He pulled me upright and kissed me. Tasting my essence on his tongue turned me on even more.

"I need you, Em," I moaned against his mouth as my hands slipped into his shorts. "Put me out of my misery..."

He was already hard as a muthafucka. It had been so long since I felt him. I was dying. He picked me up and I directed him to my room. He laid me on the bed and continued to kiss me as he finished undressing. I stared at his body, mentally taking all of him in again. He was such a beautiful specimen. His smooth chocolate skin. His chiseled abs. That long, thick ass dick with veins bulging from it. My mouth watered as I stared at him. Fuck, I had missed him. When he was fully undressed he joined me in the bed.

"I missed you so much, Rhyon," he whispered as he kissed my neck.

"I missed you, too," I breathed wrapping my arms and legs around him. I could feel the tip of his dick poking at my entrance. The moment he eased all of those inches inside of me, I lost my breath and didn't find it for about thirty seconds as he started slowly stroking me.

"Damn, Rhyon," he moaned biting his lip. "She still curves to this dick."

He hooked one of his arms under the bend of my knee and stroked me harder but kept the same pace. Every time the tip of his dick kissed my cervix, I moaned louder and louder. The louder I got, the deeper his strokes became. They were so powerful that tears began leaking from my eyes. He expertly fed me every inch of him.

"Emerald," I moaned as I dug my nails into his back and bit his collarbone.

"I love you, Rhyon," he groaned in my ear. "I love you so fucking much."

"I love you, too. I never stopped loving you."

That seemed to be all he needed to hear. He picked up his pace and dug my shit out. The bedroom was filled with the sounds of our moans and bodies slapping against each other.

"FUCK!" I cried, feeling myself about to succumb to his powerful blows. He was about to make me come undone. I thrusted my hips forward to meet him in his final strokes before we both collided in orgasmic bliss. He moaned my name loudly as I screamed his in return. He laid on top of me panting as he stared into my eyes, coming to terms with what had just happened. A smile greeted me and he kissed me softly before rolling off of me and pulling me into his arms and I nestled where I would eventually sleep peacefully for the rest of the night.

4

merald

IT HADN'T BEEN my intention to sleep over last night. Hell, it really hadn't been my intention to sleep with Rhyon at all. I honestly went over just to talk to her and bury the tension between us. The revelation of her being pregnant by me a few years ago, really sent me for a loop. Our baby would have been at least four going on five, had it survived. To think...there could have been a little mini me walking around in the world. It was killing me knowing that it was probably all the stress she was under during that time that caused her to lose the baby in the first place. I had always wanted a family with Rhyon. And now to know that had been a reality back then just wasn't sitting right with me.

I looked over at her sleeping peacefully next to me. My fingers trailed over her soft skin. My thumb traced the outline of those pouty lips that had always propelled me to kiss her whenever she bit down on them. I loved this woman to no end. She was so fucking beautiful.

So perfect. There was no way I could afford to fuck this up this time. I leaned over and kissed her lips softly. She stirred but remained asleep.

I eased out of bed and reached for my phone. It was around ten-thirty. Deciding to cook us some breakfast, I slipped on my boxers and went into the kitchen. While I got everything out I checked my messages and emails. There were a few from my manager updating me on my schedule changes. A few from my producer letting me know that he had beats for me for my next album. I had been working on a couple of songs before I left, so maybe I would do some writing while I was here.

I started cooking a breakfast of French toast, eggs and sausage. I was almost done when Rhyon came around the corner yawning. She had slipped into her robe and pulled her hair up into a bun.

"Good morning," she said coming over to me. She stood on her tip toes and kissed me sweetly.

"Good morning beautiful," I said with a smile. "How did you sleep?"

"Like a damn rock. You really wore me out last night." She giggled.

"Then I did my job," I said turning back to the stove. She came behind me and wrapped her arms around my waist. I felt her lips kissing my back and shoulders.

"I'm happy you're here, Emerald," she whispered resting her head on my back.

"Me too baby," I said trying to hold back the wave of emotions I was feeling being like this with her. "I could get use to waking up to you again, Rhyon."

"It would take a lot for that to happen," she said pulling away.

"Like what?" I asked scraping the eggs onto a plate.

"I've made a life for myself here, Emerald. I'm going great at my firm and I am up for partner. The youngest and only Black woman to do so in years."

"And I'm beyond proud of you for that, Rhyon. I knew you were destined for great things. And I will always support that. I just want you with me."

"I'm not quitting my job."

"I'm not asking you to do that," I said turning to put the plates on the counter. I remembered our little sexcapade on the countertop and moved everything to the kitchen table. She took a seat and I grabbed our drinks.

"Then how is this going to work? I can't do long distance again, Emerald. That killed us the last time. And I know you aren't going to give up your career so I can practice law here. I wouldn't even think to ask you to do that."

"What if I could offer you something?" I asked sitting a glass of orange juice down in front of her and taking my seat. "A compromise."

"A compromise?"

"Come work for me."

"I'm not an entertainment lawyer, Emerald. I practice criminal defense."

"I know that. Which is why the entertainment industry is perfect for you. Do you know how many Hollywood scandals have been covered up over the decades? People will pay big bucks to make some shit go away or make sure it never reaches the public. Sometimes your career is only as strong as your legal team. I've been following you over the years, Rhyon. You know your shit. You have been killing it since before you passed the bar."

"But who in Hollywood is going to hire a small-town girl from South Carolina? That is the big leagues compared to here. I can't go out there and fall flat on my face."

"You won't fall flat on your face. You've got me..."

"That's what I'm talking about, Emerald. I don't want to fall back on you. I'm twenty-seven years old. I don't need you to take care of me. I told you before and I will tell you again, I refuse to ride your coattails."

"How is it riding my coattails, Rhyon? If we are together..."

"But we aren't together!"

"Will you please just hear me out? Please?"

She sighed and cut into her French toast. I took her silence as permission to continue.

"Rhyon, if we are together, I am your partner. We are a team. A package deal. What's mine is yours. If I am in a position to help you, let me do that. I would never take away from everything you accomplished on your own. You rightfully earned that shit and I would stand ten toes down to make sure everybody knows that you got here because of *you*." I reached for her hand and she hesitantly took mine.

"I owe you baby," I said. "You are the reason that I have the success that I have."

"How? I wasn't even around."

"But you were. When I said I carried you in my spirit, I meant that. You know what your father said to me yesterday? That you didn't sing with as much emotion as I did without actually feeling that shit. Every top selling single I have is because of you. You were my muse baby. When I stepped into that studio, I let all of you lose in that booth. Everything I ever felt for you went into those lyrics. Everything I ever *wanted* from you. Everything I ever needed. It's always been you."

She kissed my hand and smiled softly.

"I appreciate that, Emerald," she said. "But it's not about accepting help from you. And the job is certainly not about the money for me. I can't sleep at night knowing that I helped get someone off free for some shit they deserved to serve time or be punished for. I want to help people. I want to make a difference. Hollywood isn't the place for me."

She pulled her hand away and went back to eating her food. The rest of our meal was silent.

 hyon

I sat in Dr. Claytor's waiting room anxious for my appointment. My anxiety had been at an all-time high since the conversation with Emerald a week ago. I was a little frustrated that he wasn't understanding why I became a lawyer in the first place. I had only been dreaming of it since I was ten. He knew my history. My father and grandfather were lawyers, both legends in their own right. I watched them both step into a courtroom and command not only the room, but respect. They could make even the toughest criminals crack under pressure.

I'd had a lot to prove during school once it became known that I was following in their footsteps. I never wanted anyone to question whether I earned my title because of them or because I put in the hard work. I worked double time to be the best in my class. My professors saw that in me. That's why after graduation, I had several offers for employment. I didn't use my father's or grandfather's name then, and I refused to use Emerald's now.

Dr. Claytor's office door opened and I stood as she said goodbye to one of her clients. When she saw me she smiled.

"Rhyon! Come on in!" she said waving me into the office. She closed the door behind me and then hugged me. We had been seeing each other so long that she had almost become like my best friend. I mean the woman knew everything about me at this point.

"To what do I owe this visit?" she asked handing me a bottle of water and taking a seat in her chair. She grabbed her notepad and a pen and crossed her legs.

"Well first thing is Emerald is back in town."

"How are you feeling about that?"

"At first, I didn't have time to take in the news. He kind of bum rushed this date I was on by paying for our dinner and then coming to sit at our table."

"I imagine that caused you some discomfort."

"Oh, yeah. Dinner was pretty much done at that point."

"How did you feel when you saw him?"

"Angry. Happy. Confused. Anxious. It was like he wanted to entice me. He followed me to the bathroom and he kissed me."

"How did you respond to that?"

"I didn't kiss him back, but the way he made my body feel, it was like he never left. Excuse me for being frank but I feel like we've been going through this for four years, so I feel comfortable enough to tell you that my pussy was throbbing after that kiss."

Dr. Claytor stifled a laugh.

"I'm serious. He told me that he came back for me and that he wasn't leaving until I was his. I don't even know how long he plans to be here."

"Those sound like intense feelings."

"That's just Emerald. When he is passionate about something, he doesn't stop until he has it. So much so that our relationship suffered for it. It's been four years since I've seen him and now I've seen him several times this past week."

"How so?"

"Well two days after I saw him at the restaurant, he was at my parents' house when I went to visit them and nobody gave me a heads up. We had an argument about our breakup and things in the past. He asked if he could see me later so that we could further discuss everything."

"And you agreed?"

I nodded. "I felt like I needed to get some things off of my chest. So I agreed."

"Well that is a great step in recovery. Letting people know how they made you feel is a therapy in itself."

"I told him about the baby," I said quietly.

She gave me a moment to process my feelings. Then she asked, "How did you feel finally disclosing that?"

"Honestly, I felt relieved to finally get it off of my chest."

"What about Emerald? How did he respond to the news?"

"He was angry that I didn't tell him I was pregnant when I found out."

"I know we have discussed this before, but now that you've told him, do you regret not saying anything back then? Do you think it would have made a difference?"

"I don't know, maybe he would have been there for me. Maybe he would have been too busy."

"Knowing him the way that you do, do you honestly feel like he would have been too busy?"

I sighed heavily. "No. I just...I loved him. I wanted to tell him that I was pregnant. I wanted to tell him about the miscarriage. I didn't want to inconvenience the moves he was making back then. His career was just taking off, I took the miscarriage hard and I would have felt guilty having him come home to babysit me."

"You were in a relationship, Rhyon. If you needed to lean on anyone, it would have been him."

"I know." I dropped my head. "I feel bad about it."

"Did you apologize?"

"No. God, through the surge of emotions I didn't even say that I was sorry. I'm so selfish."

I dropped my head in my hands and started to cry. I felt fucked up about that. Emerald had comforted me and I hadn't genuinely acknowledged his feelings at all. He apologized for not being there even when I didn't give him a chance to. Dr. Claytor came and sat next to me with a box of tissues. She handed me one and gently rubbed my back as I tried to get myself together.

"I'm sorry, I'm such a mess," I said wiping my face.

"No apologies needed. That's what you have me for, remember?" She offered me a smile and a warm hug and then went back to her chair. "So tell me about the rest of his visit."

"Well," I said nervously rubbing the back of my neck, "things kind of took a turn."

"Meaning?"

"We might have slept together."

"Might have?"

"Okay, we did. I couldn't help myself. I haven't gotten laid in six months and he hasn't touched me in four years. When he started singing to me, I don't know. I came undone. He took me right there in my kitchen."

"What are your feelings about having sex with him?"

"I mean, it was perfect. It was so much better than old times. Even though I'm sure he's been with other women since me and I've been with other men since him, it was like our bodies were speaking to each other. Like he just knew what I needed. I don't regret it."

"Have there been any talks of you two reconciling?"

"He maintains that he wants me with him. I told him I can't just quit my job. Then he offers for me to come work for him."

"That was very generous."

"As generous as it was I turned him down. I'm not an entertainment lawyer. I specialize in criminal defense. I don't care how much he could pay me or how much his industry friends could pay me. I want to help justice be served. I don't want to cover up crimes of the rich and famous."

"Well I applaud you for sticking to your guns. I know working a fulfilling career is important to you, Rhyon."

"It is. I thought he would understand that."

"I wouldn't say he doesn't understand it. I think he just wants to offer you security. What would it take for you to be with him again?"

I sat there for the longest time trying to find the answer to that question. Other than the issue with my job, what else would it take to be with Emerald? I loved him, but did I trust him to put me first this time? Could I handle being away from him when he was on tour? Would this distance kill us yet again?

"I don't know," I finally answered. "I love him, but it's just not enough."

"I have an assignment for you," she said ripping out a piece of paper.

I sat up as she wrote something down. She handed me the paper.

"In the four years that I have known you, I think I have a pretty good feeling about where your heart is, Rhyon. I just want you to be sure. You have loved this man for half of your life. Your anxieties stem from your breakup and you need to confront that before you two can ever move forward, if that is what you want. You are operating on fear right now. So, for two weeks, I want you to write down all the pros and cons that you can think of in regards to being with Emerald. How he makes you feel. How being without him makes you feel. Good and bad things. In that time, I want you do sit down and have a serious conversation with him because I don't think you have fully expressed all of your feelings to him. You said yourself that it's been four years."

"Pros and cons? You think two weeks is long enough?"

Dr. Claytor chuckled. "If I know you like I think I do, you will excel at this exercise."

I looked down at the paper.

Pros and cons.

Good and bad.

"What do I do if the bad outweighs the good?"

"If the bad outweighs the good then you have nothing to lose. But if the good outweighs the bad, you have to seriously think about your future and your happiness. What is it that *you* want?"

I nodded and tucked the paper into my purse. This was going to be a hell of an exercise.

 merald

"WAS I wrong to offer her a job, Ma?" I asked sitting in my parents' living room after dinner.

"You want my honest opinion, Em?" she asked, sipping her glass of wine.

"Yes ma'am."

She took another sip and then sat the glass down and looked at me.

"You weren't wrong, but you may have come off as selfish."

"Selfish?"

"Baby, Rhyon has always been fiercely independent. She's worked hard to prove herself not only outside of her father and grandfather's legacies but as a strong and educated Black woman. For you to offer her a job, as noble as it was, it wasn't the right move. If you want her to be with you, you have to invest in her. Invest in her dream. Show her that you support her career like she supported yours. That girl was at every talent show, every audition, gig and studio session you had before you left. She listened when you needed a critic. She held your hand whether you won or if you took a loss. She was right there."

"I know, Ma," I said tossing my head back on the couch. "I can't spend the rest of my life without her. I love that woman with my soul, Ma."

"I know you do baby. But it's been four years since you broke up. You can't come in and throw your money at her and expect her to fall at your feet."

"That's not what I intended to do. I just want to give her an opportunity to do what she loves and we still have a life together."

"Then you need to figure out how to do that. Compromise isn't as complicated as it's made out to be."

She picked up her wine glass and went into the kitchen to help my father wash the dishes. I watched them be so loving and playful even after all these years. They adored each other. Rhyon's parents were the same way. They had been a shining example of what I wanted in my own marriage. Not to say that they didn't have their share of problems, because they did. No marriage was perfect. But I had watched these two couples maintain the love they had shared for over two decades.

That's what I was trying to do with Rhyon.

I had loved her since I was in second grade. I know you're thinking what does an eight-year-old know about true love. But I felt that shit the moment I laid eyes on her standing in front of our class with her cute little white dress and big white bow in her hair. She looked just like a little chocolate barbie doll back then. And now she was a beautiful, strong, and sexy full-grown woman that enticed me at my very core.

She didn't need me, but I needed her and more than that, I needed her to want me as bad as I wanted her.

I DECIDED to surprise Rhyon at work with lunch. I hadn't seen her since the night we made love. We had been talking and texting for the last couple of weeks but she wouldn't allow me to see her again. Recently our conversations had been brief. I missed her. So after my work out and shower, I slipped into a pair of black, skinny, dress jeans, a green polo shirt and a comfortable pair of sneakers. I decided to forgo the flashy jewelry I normally wore a simple pair of studs, a gold chain, and my watch. I sprayed myself with her favorite cologne and headed out.

Rhyon worked for a prominent law firm in the city. When I stepped inside, I took in the atmosphere and the vibe. It just looked like a place that got down to business and that is exactly what my baby did.

My baby? There I went claiming her again. I shook the thought from my head and approached the tall, brown skin sista with a big curly afro sitting at the receptionist desk.

"Excuse me, Jessica?" I said reading her name tag.

She looked up and her eyes widened.

"You...you're...YOU'RE GEM!" she whispered loudly. I could tell she was a fan. I smiled.

"Yes, I am."

"Oh my gosh, I'm your biggest fan. I just love you! Your voice is so beautiful! You just sing to my soul! I have all of your albums!" she smiled brightly.

"Well thank you. I appreciate that."

"Could I bother you for an autograph, maybe a picture?"

"It's no problem. I'm always happy to meet a homegrown fan."

She eagerly rounded the desk with her phone and we posed for a few pictures. I then signed her autograph and she went back to her workstation.

"Whew!" she said shaking her hands. "Okay, now that I'm done fangirling, how can I help you?"

"Would you be so kind as to point me in the direction of Rhyon Capers?"

"Just a moment." She typed on her keyboard and then picked up the phone and dialed a number.

"Ms. Capers you have a visitor," she said in a more professional tone. "A certain gentleman." She smiled at me. "Yes ma'am. Okay." She hung up. "She said she'll be down in five minutes."

"Thank you so much." I smiled. She giggled. I took a seat in the lobby and waited for Rhyon to come down. I ended up signing a few more autographs and taking a few pictures. When I saw Rhyon step off of the elevator on her phone , I excused myself from the small crowd and made my way to her. She looked beautiful in this red dress that made me envious of how it hugged her curves. It stopped right above her knees showing off those legs that had been wrapped around my shoulders and waist a few weeks ago. On her feet were a pair of nude heels. Her braids were done in a bun and she wore simple silver accessories.

I licked my lips as we approached each other.

She ended the call and gave me her attention.

"Hey beautiful," I said reaching for her hand and kissing it. I pulled her into my embrace and kissed her cheek.

"Hey Emerald." She smiled. "What are you doing here?"

"I thought I would take you to lunch, if you're feeling up to that."

"Actually, that would be nice. I've been working on this case all morning and I'm starving."

"Perfect. I've been dying to go to *Iris'* since I touched down," I said referring to what use to be our favorite hangout spot.

"That would hit the spot!" she said, her eyes beaming as she rubbed her stomach. "I can almost taste that chicken philly."

"You still love those, huh?"

"Boy those never lose flavor! Ms. Iris sees my face once a week. I don't even have to tell her what I want."

"You think she'll remember me?"

"How could she forget you? We celebrated you getting signed right at her diner. She even named your favorite dish after you."

"She did?"

"She did. I'm sure she'll be happy to see you after all this time."

I smiled. Iris Taylor was the neighborhood grandmother that ran one of the first Black-owned diners in the city. There was so much history in that place. Rhyon, Melissa and I practically lived in there during high school.

"I can't wait to see her," I said. "Do you need to grab anything before we go?"

"Nope."

"Well let's go feed our faces then," I said offering her my arm. She slipped hers through mine and I escorted her out of the building. When we pulled up to the diner, memories came flooding back. The amount of time we spent here was ridiculous. This was the spot back in the day. I had performed here so many times for amateur night. This was where Rhyon and I shared our first kiss. I could feel her eyes on me as I put the car in park.

"Brings back memories doesn't it?" she asked.

"Oh yea," I said opening my door. I walked around to the passenger side and opened hers, offering her my hand.

"Thank you," she said lacing her fingers through mine. It was a small gesture, but it held a magnitude of intimacy for me. We walked hand in hand into the diner. Before the door closed, Ms. Iris spotted us.

"Oh my lord!" she said coming from behind the counter. It was a wonder my damn jaws weren't hurting as hard as I was smiling when she approached me. "As I live and breathe! Emerald Hampton! It's so good to see you baby!" She scooped me up in one of those hugs that only a church lady could give you.

"It's good to see you too, Ms. Iris," I said hugging her back.

"Hey Rhyon baby," she said hugging her when she released me.

"Hey, Ms. Iris."

"It's so good to see you two back together. I always knew you had something special."

"Oh we're not together," Rhyon said letting go of my hand but holding onto my arm. "Emerald is just in town for a while and decided to take me to lunch."

"Well that's a bummer." She frowned. "I always thought you two made a beautiful couple. Don't mind me though. Come and have a seat."

She led us to the corner booth we always sat in whenever we came here and sat with us.

"How long are you in town for, Emerald?" she asked.

"I'm not sure. It could be a while."

"The spotlight becoming too much for you? You know you use to tear my stage up with that voice of yours."

"I remember." I laughed. "But no, I can deal with the spotlight." I looked at Rhyon. "I came back for something special though."

Ms. Iris smiled. "Well I hope it works out. Lord knows you've been singing to this girl long enough. You better claim your man, Rhyon. Life is too short to be anything but happy." She slid out of the booth.

"Now," she said putting her hands on her hips. "Chicken Philly with fries and extra ranch dressing on the side for you," she said, pointing at Rhyon. "And for you...the hot dog basket with fries and a side of honey garlic wings, extra crispy, extra sauce on the side."

"You know us well," I said with a smile.

"Of course I do," she said cupping my chin then kissing my cheek. "I'll be back with your order shortly."

She left us alone. Rhyon moved away from me slightly. I could tell she was in her thoughts by the way she was biting her bottom lip and pretending to play with her nails. It was always a nervous habit for her.

"Something on your mind?" I asked.

"A lot," she answered. She finally looked at me. "I need to say something to you, Emerald."

"What is it?" I asked throwing my arm around the back of the booth.

"I need to apologize to you."

"For?"

"For keeping my pregnancy and miscarriage a secret."

"Rhyon..."

"No, let me say this." She took a deep breath. "When you left, I had a hard time dealing with it. So many times I wanted to ask you to just come home. Leave behind everything and come back to me. And I realize how selfish that was, which is why I never did it. I didn't know how to live without you, Emerald. Maybe that was an unhealthy attachment but it was how I felt. So much of our lives were wrapped up in and surrounded by each other. I had to learn who I was outside of you and I understand now that you did too. When I found out that I was pregnant, I didn't want to distract you. You were just getting your career off the ground and I didn't want to be the reason you missed your big break. I knew eventually I had to tell you. I was going to tell you..."

She swallowed hard as her eyes glistened with tears.

"When I miscarried, I was in a bad space. I needed you and I was afraid to reach out to you. I felt guilty about asking you to come home and basically babysit me. I didn't give you the credit you deserved as my man, as father of my child to think that you would *want* to be there for me. I'm sorry that I made that decision for you. I was wrong and I hope that you can forgive me for being so selfish and inconsiderate."

I was surprised to say the least. I sat there for minutes, quietly processing what she had said. She looked at me anxiously, waiting for me to say something.

"Thank you, Rhyon," I finally said.

"I needed to say that. My therapist asked me if I had apologized..."

"Therapist?"

"Yes," she hesitated. "I have been seeing her since our breakup. I've been dealing with anxiety for the last couple of years, Emerald. It started with my insecurity of not having you in my life and it spilled over into other things. Sometimes I get so overwhelmed. Dr. Claytor says that it's high functioning but mentally...it fucks with me."

"How are you feeling right now?"

"I feel okay. You just...you still entice my senses, Emerald." She turned and angled her body towards mine. Her fingers gently trace my bottom lip. "When I'm with you, all my defenses just break down. The anger I felt for you just dissipates and all I can feel is how much I still love you. How much I still want you. I can't fight that."

"Then don't fight it, Rhyon," I said gently gripping her wrist. I kissed her fingertips.

"I'm afraid, Emerald," she whispered, tears slipping from her eyes.

"You don't have to be afraid of me baby." I slid closer to her. "You don't have to be afraid of loving me and letting me love you because that's all we have ever done. I've loved you since I was eight years old. Back when you wore those church dresses, big ass bows, and those frilly ass socks with the token white shoes."

She giggled at the memory.

"We grew together, Rhyon. We saw each other through the worst and the best. I made a mistake in leaving you behind. You were my biggest blessing and I fumbled your heart when you entrusted it to me. You were right. I did get too busy for you. I was grinding so hard trying to make it in the industry that I forgot that I owed you my respect, my loyalty, my security. I ignored my gut when it came to sensing that you needed me. I told myself that it was just me missing you and that I needed to shake it off and keep it pushing. When you left me, it broke me. For all the times I tried to reach out to you after you blocked me, it never crossed my mind to just come home and make things right. I didn't know how to fix it without risking hurting you again and I couldn't bear to do that. So I just let it go, or so I thought. I thought about you every single day, Rhyon. I prayed for you every day. I asked God to take care of you until I could be there to take care of you myself. I asked him to take care of your heart, because even though I had broken it, I needed him to hold those pieces until I could put it back together."

She squeezed my hand. I reached out to wipe the tears from her beautiful face.

"I want to be with you baby," I said. "What do I have to do to have that? What do you need from me, right now at this very moment?"

"Kiss me," she pleaded.

I was more than willing to oblige her. I pulled her face to mine and lowered my lips to hers. It was a soft, sensual kiss at first. Innocent, yet filled with so much passion. I slipped my tongue into her mouth and she wrestled with it for dominance before finally allowing me to take control. I felt her body relax against mine

"I love you, Emerald," she whispered against my mouth, pressing her forehead against mine.

"I love you, too," I said cupping her face. I kissed her nose and buried my face in her neck. She smelled divine. Like a mixture between honey and peaches and cream. I pulled away from her and stared at her. Not a single word was spoken between us until Ms. Iris brought over our food. She was smiling big as Rhyon and I pulled ourselves away from each other.

"My babies," she sang sitting our plates down.

Rhyon and I just smiled at her.

"You know I still have the amateur nights here Emerald," she said. "Even though there is nothing amateur about you, I would love it if you came and sang for the crowd Saturday night."

"Anything for you baby," I said taking her hand and kissing it. She blushed and waved me off.

"Oh stop it," she giggled. "You are gonna give an old woman a heart attack."

"You know you've always been one of my favorite girls, Ms. Iris."
I laughed. "I'll be here. Same time?"

"Same time." She kissed my forehead. "I'll leave you two to your
meal. Don't be dry humping in my booth now."

"Ms. Iris!" Rhyon exclaimed as she giggled.

"Don't 'Ms. Iris' me! I saw you two exchanging saliva over here.
You may not be together, but your hearts are with each other. You'll
work it out. That I have faith in."

She winked at us and then walked away.

We dug into our food and the rest of our lunch date was peaceful.
We laughed and talked and reminisced about old times at this place.
Before we left, Ms. Iris gave us two slices of her famous sweet potato
pie. Even though she wouldn't allow me to pay our bill, I slipped her
a hefty tip just for being the sweetheart she had always been.

Rhyon and I rode back to her office jamming to old school music
and cutting up in my car. When we pulled up to the building I wasn't
ready to let her go. I held on to her hand, caressing it with my thumb.

"What is it?" she asked smiling lovingly at me.

"I'm not ready to leave you," I said truthfully.

"This doesn't have to be goodbye," she said quietly. "You could
come over tonight."

"I would like that."

She leaned over and pulled my face to hers. The kiss she gave me
damn near made my toes curl. My dick bricked the fuck up as she
sucked on my bottom lip.

"Mmm...you better stop doing that before you don't make it back
to work," I mumbled against her mouth.

She giggled as she pulled away from me.

"I'll see you tonight, Emerald."

"You most definitely will," I said biting my lip. I watched her climb
out of my truck, taking the opportunity to slap that ass as she did.

She shook her head and started into the building. I rolled down
the window and called her name.

"Rhyon!"

"What?"

"I love you."

She smiled. "I love you too, Emerald," she said before heading back inside. I sat there for a moment, basking in how good that shit felt. How right it felt. This was going to work this time. I could feel it.

Rhyon

I WALKED BACK into my office with a slight bounce in my step. Lunch with Emerald had been wonderful. The more time I spent with him, the easier it was to allow the feelings I shared for him to resurface. When we were together everything felt right about being with him, even when it was going wrong. We had both grown over the years and our communication with each other had gotten better even with him just coming back around. The conversations we had been having were open and honest. We allowed ourselves to be vulnerable with each other and in return it opened up a whole new level of intimacy.

I sat at my desk looking over the list the Dr. Claytor was having me compile. It had been two weeks to the day. So far I had at least twenty things under the pros list and only three under the cons. While it would seem like a no brainer, the things I had listed were major. Number one, could I trust him again? It would be easy to say that I had trusted him enough to give my body again, why not my heart?

Number two, was I prepared to live the lifestyle he did? I didn't like the spotlight. I wasn't sure if I could deal with the cameras all in my face, the constant pressure to look like I was gonna hit the runway at any given time or thot ass bitches throwing themselves at my man. I knew it came with the territory but I was a behind the scenes kind of woman. I was the woman that was your peace from the outside world, at least that was what I wanted to be for him.

Number three, if I had to, could I live without him for good? That was the most pressing question. Could I go through the rest of my life accepting that the kind of love we shared was only supposed to be for a season and not for a lifetime? I knew I couldn't. Everything that was Emerald Davis Hampton was supposed to be mine. To have and to hold. For richer or poorer. In sickness and in health. I laughed at myself for referencing marriage vows right now. But it was how I felt. That man was supposed to be my husband.

I knew it. He knew it. Everybody knew it.

We just had to figure out how to make it work this time.

My thoughts were interrupted by the sound of my phone ringing. It was Melissa.

"Hello?" I answered.

"Biiiiitch!" she squealed.

"What?"

"Tell me why there is a picture of you and Emerald slobbing each other down in *Iris'*!"

"What the fuck! We literally just left there like fifteen minutes ago, Melissa."

"Girl you know these people work fast."

I pulled the phone from my ear and searched for it. Sure enough, there we were, getting hot and heavy in that back booth with the caption, *"I guess he wants that old thing back!"* The picture already had several thousand shares. I could only imagine the number of shares it would have by morning.

"Ain't this some shit," I mumbled.

"Don't sweat it girl." She laughed. "It ain't a secret that you and Emerald dated to anybody around here. *However...*" she said stressing the word. "How dare your black ass keep this juiciness from me! Your best friend! I'm hurt."

"Shut the fuck up, Melissa," I said rolling my eyes.

"I'm serious! You kissing on him like you done fucked the man... did you get some dick Rhyon?" she asked.

"Bye Melissa!"

"Ain't no damn *'Bye Melissa.'* Don't you hang up on me!" she said. "I swear to God, I will take this elevator down to your floor with a quickness!"

I knew she would. That was just how crazy she was. I worked on the fourth floor and Melissa, coincidently worked on the twelfth.

"I need the tea," she said. "Sooo... you can either give it to me now, or I can bring my pretty ass downstairs and we can do it in person...as a matter of fact, I'll see you in five."

She hung up and I shook my head as I sat my phone down. That girl was crazy. Maybe I did need to talk to her about everything. She would be honest with me and tell me if I was making a mistake. I needed someone to tell me that I wasn't tripping.

Exactly five minutes later, Melissa came barging into my office with a grin on her face. She closed my door and sat down in the chair across from me.

"Spill it," she said.

"Well good afternoon to you too," I said turning to her from my email.

"Rhyon don't play with me."

I sighed. "Okay, okay...we had sex."

She squealed so loud that it caused the secretary walking by to stop and look in the window. I assured her that everything was okay with a wave of my hand and pulled the shades down.

"Why are you so damn extra?" I asked shaking my head.

"I'm just excited!"

"About me getting some dick?"

"Yes! Rhyon you been fronting for years like you didn't still love that man. It's been worse since he came back to town. I was wondering how long it was going to take for him to break that ass down. You could have had him back a long time ago."

"I don't know that I have him now…"

"What? Girl the man came back for you. He put his career on hold to pursue you with no interference."

"I don't know, Melissa." I looked over at the list I had been making for Dr. Claytor. Now was as good a time as any to tell her my secret. I handed her the paper. She laughed as she read over it.

"Really, Rhyon? You are making lists…"

"It's actually something my therapist recommended…"

The smile dropped from her face. "Therapist?"

"I've been seeing her the last couple of years."

"The last couple of years? What's going on, Rhyon?"

I took a deep breath and told her everything. And I mean everything. By the time I was done, we were both crying. She got up from her chair and came to sit on my lap and hug me.

"You could have told me, baby," she cried. "I would have been right there with you. You're my best friend, practically my sister. Don't you know that I would do anything for you girl?"

"I know," I said wiping my face. "I just didn't know how to process it all. So I didn't. I just put it on the back burner. The problem with that is that it just kept boiling and spilling over."

"Listen to me," she said moving from my lap to sit on top of my desk. "I love you. Emerald loves you. And you love him. You don't need to make a list to figure out what you already know. Just be with him, Rhyon."

"How am I supposed to just give up my whole life to follow around a man?"

"You wouldn't be giving up your life. You would be starting your next chapter. And let's be real. Emerald isn't just any man. He's the one that is supposed to be yours baby. It's always been him, it will always be him. Everything that you want, you can have with him. Love, your career, happiness and yes, marriage and children. I hate that you lost your baby, but maybe that was a sign that you two weren't ready at that exact moment. Maybe you two needed this time apart to grow and discover how much you really mean to each other so when you came back together you would be stronger."

"So you think I should give him a chance?"

"Yes bitch!" She playfully mushed me. "Look at it like this. You did everything that you set out to do when you stayed behind. You got your degree. You work for the top law firm in the state. You're making a difference. You have made your mark all on your own. I say throw caution to the wind."

"I still want to work, Melissa. I don't want Emerald's money."

"Rhyon, you can practice law anywhere. Hell, you could open your own practice."

"Really?"

"Yes really. You're great at what you do. You're passionate and determined and so fucking smart. You would thrive out there, all those damn criminals," she added with a laugh.

"How could I ever leave you behind?"

"Oh baby you aren't leaving me. Hopping on a plane to see you ain't shit. Besides, you are gonna be knocked up in no time if you move. TeTe has to see her babies!"

"Not you over here speaking to my womb."

"I speak it in abundance!" She threw up her hands and pretended to speak in tongues and I died laughing.

"You are a fool!"

"And you know this! But you love me anyway."

"That I do," I said grabbing her hands. "Thank you, Melissa," I said standing.

"Anytime girl." She kissed my cheek and pulled me into a hug. "So, I have a question for you. Totally off topic." She reclaimed her chair, as did I.

"Shoot."

"Would it be weird if I asked Chad out?"

"Chad?"

"Yea...we've been talking and I know you guys had that whole date and whatnot but I really like him, Rhyon..."

"It's totally fine, Melissa." I smiled.

"You sure? It wouldn't be awkward?"

"Girl no. Chad is a good guy. He just wasn't for me. If you like him, go for it."

"Really?"

"Absolutely. Besides, I told him you would be setting him up again in no time."

She laughed. "I just didn't think that it would be with *me*."

"Funny how that works. I hope he is everything you are looking for."

"I have a good feeling about it. I mean I've worked with him for two years. He's always been so respectful and down to earth. I hope he can handle my crazy ass."

"I'm sure he will tame the raging beast inside of you."

"Girl I bet that dick will do wonders for this attitude!" She stuck out her tongue and twerked a little.

"I can't with you."

"Let me get my ass back upstairs before they come looking for me," she said, standing. "You better let me know how things go."

"I will."

"I love you, boo."

"I love you too, crazy girl."

I MADE it to my house around six thirty. I had called Emerald when I got off and he was there waiting for me when I pulled into my driveway. He stepped out of his car wearing a tank top, joggers and slides, and made his way to my driver's side door.

"Hey beautiful," he said as he helped me out. He took my bags and kissed my cheek.

"Hey handsome." I smiled lacing my fingers through his. We ascended up the walkway to my front door and I unlocked it to let us in. I motioned for him to put my things down by the door and I would grab them later.

"How was your day?" he asked pulling me into his arms.

"It was good. I had lunch with this fine ass brotha that kissed me like he missed me," I said, sliding my arms around his waist.

"Anybody I know?" He grinned cupping my chin. His lips greeted mine and I wanted to melt. Emerald's kisses always made me weak in the knees. His tongue slipped in my mouth and a moan slipped from my lips as he grabbed my ass.

"Mmm," I moaned pressing my body against his. He picked me up and wrapped my legs around his waist.

"Don't you drop me." I giggled in between kisses.

"I got this." He slapped my ass. I squealed in excitement.

"I need to shower first."

"Well let's get you wet then."

"I think I'm already there," I said seductively as he carried me into my bedroom. When we got inside he undressed me from head to toe, strategically placing kisses on my skin.

"What did you do after lunch?" I asked walking into the bathroom butt ass naked.

"I had a few meetings I needed to take care of. But for the most part, I just chilled with my folks. Trying to spend as much time with them as possible before I leave."

I could hear the sadness in his voice as I came to the bathroom door.

"You really missed them, huh?" I said.

"I did. Being back home, surrounded by all this love from people who really know me, I've missed it. Don't get me wrong, I love singing. I love making music and seeing people enjoy something I created but sometimes I just miss home."

"What do you think you would be doing if you hadn't chosen to sing professionally?"

"Honestly, I can't picture me doing anything else. I feel like it's something that I was meant to do. My purpose." He looked at me. "Like you being a lawyer. Do you think you could see yourself doing anything else?"

"No. I can't. I've wanted this for as long as I can remember. If I couldn't do that...I don't think I would be me."

"I get that now," he said, looking down. "I realize how important it was for you to do something for yourself, by yourself. I'm sorry if I ever made you feel like you had to choose. I also want to apologize if it seemed like I was throwing my money at you when I offered you a job. My intentions were good, they just came off the wrong way. For that I am sorry."

I walked over to him, still in all my naked glory and cupped his face. "All is forgiven, Emerald," I said. "I want to talk to you about something when I get out of the shower, okay?"

"Okay." I pecked his lips and hurried to go wash my ass. When I got out of the shower, I sat at my vanity, moisturizing my skin. I let my hair down and slipped into my silk robe and left the bathroom. Emerald had kicked off his slides and was laid out across my bed sleeping softly. I stood in the doorway just watching him with a smile on my face. I could get use to coming home to him at night again. Waking up to him again. Making love to him until my body ached from all the pleasure he brought me.

I made my way over to the bed and climbed on top of him. I kissed the corners of his mouth and then made my way to his neck. He stirred slightly but remained asleep. The man had always been a hard sleeper. I had something to wake his ass up though. I made my way down to the waistband of his joggers and slowly maneuvered them and his boxers down over his hips.

I took his dick in my hands and began stroking him. He moaned softly. Even though he was asleep, he was at full attention in no time. I was about to wake his ass right the fuck up. I ran my tongue from the base of his dick all the way to the head and swirled my tongue around it. Letting the spit from my mouth drip down his shaft, I took him into its wetness.

"Mmm..." he moaned, stirring again.

I slurped his dick all the way to the back of my throat, maintaining my gag reflexes. As I sucked him, I used my hand to jack him off in the process. I gripped the base of his dick tightly as I stroked and sucked him at the same time.

"Damn, Rhyon," he moaned, finally sitting up on his elbows. Now that he was awake, I was really going to put on a show for him. I sucked his dick like I owed him money. Between the movement of my hands and the suction of my jaws, he was moaning and groaning and calling my name.

"Fuck! Goddammit Rhyon, suck that shit baby," he said gripping a hand full of my braids. I looked up at him as I continued my assault. He loved that shit. I rested my hands on his thighs and sucked him deep into my mouth, coating his shit with my spit. At this point he was getting some nasty, sloppy ass head.

"Shit!" he said loudly as he bit his lip.

I maneuvered myself into position and slid my pussy down onto his dick.

"You're so wet baby," he moaned gripping my thighs. I pulled the sash on my robe and let it fall from my shoulders, exposing my hardened nipples. He sat up and latched on to one as he played with the other between his thumb and forefinger.

"Emerald," I moaned tossing my head back.

"Damn, I love you, Rhyon," he said lightly gripping my throat.

"Oooo, I love you, too," I pushed him down and rested my hands on either side of his head. I leaned forward and kissed him as I continued to ride him. He gripped my ass and thrusted his hips into me.

"What do you want from me, Emerald?" I asked breathlessly. "Tell me again, baby."

"I want you to be mine," he moaned. He sank his teeth into my shoulder and I cried out in pleasure.

"Shit! What else?" I moaned.

"I want you with me. None of this shit means anything if I don't have you, Rhyon. You are my world baby. My heart in human form. I look at you and I see perfection, something imperfectly made just for me. I love you with everything that is in me."

He flipped me over onto my back and commanded control of my body as he fed me inch by inch of him. My breath caught in my throat with every stroke. He covered my mouth with his and kissed me passionately.

"I can give you the world baby," he whispered. "Let me make all of your dreams come true. Whatever I have to do to have you, it's yours..."

"Fuck," I moaned as his strokes deepened. I clung to him as he continued to speak to me.

"I want to grow old with you, Rhyon," he said, looking deep into my eyes. "I want to marry you and raise a family with you. I want to give you the life we were always meant to have together. Let me do that for you baby."

"Yes..." I whispered. "God yes..."

I pulled his head to mine and kissed him wildly. I felt my body begin to tremble. My orgasm was rising and I could feel myself coming undone.

"I love you," he moaned.

"I love you too...so fucking much. SHIT!"

I pulled his body close to mine, digging my nails into his back as I came.

"Emerald!" I screamed.

He gave me a final thrust before I felt his seed shooting off deep inside of me. We laid in each other's arms, trying to catch our breaths and come down from the natural high we were on. He looked down at me, pushing my braids from my sweat covered brow.

"Just so we are clear, that was a yes, right?" he asked.

I couldn't help but laugh. "That was a definite yes." I giggled.

He gripped the back of my neck and kissed me with so much love and passion.

This felt right.

Finally, it felt right.

EPILOGUE

ight months later

I EASED into the comfortable plush chair behind my desk in my new office. Looking around at the journey I was about to step in made my heart swell. Everything that had transpired in the last eight months all led up to this moment.

The law offices of Rhyon Capers-Hampton Esq. were now open for business.

It was bittersweet leaving the job I had worked at for the last couple of years. My boss was sad to see me go but was proud that I was venturing out on my own. He even promised to recommend me to several people he knew out west. That I was grateful for.

Emerald had kept his word in doing whatever he needed to get me to come all the way out here with him. When I told him I wanted to open my own firm, he jumped right in and made that happen. He put me in contact with his realtor and a contractor and told me to have at it, just send him the bill. It meant the world to me to have him invest in my dream. To see my vision and make it a reality.

We got married shortly before we left South Carolina. Nothing huge, just a small intimate ceremony at the church we grew up in with our families and closest friends and of course Dr. Claytor. It was beautiful. Walking down that aisle with my father towards the man that was always meant to be my husband, was like walking into a new life. I had never been so happy.

During our reception, I had pulled Dr. Claytor aside and thanked her for all she had done for me over the years. I didn't know it at the time, but the list of pros and cons she had me create was intended to help me put things into perspective. I was an overthinker and she understood that about me. Having me write down my honest and true thoughts and fears helped me come to terms with my truest feeling. It made me see what I stood to lose versus what I stood to gain.

She had simply smiled and told me she knew that I would make the best decision for myself and she was just there to give me a little push.

A knock on my door interrupted my thoughts.

"Come in," I said.

The door opened and in walked my husband with a bouquet of my favorite flowers. I smiled as I stood to greet him and take the flowers. After sniffing them I placed them on my desk.

"Mrs. Hampton, what a pleasure it is to lay eyes and hands on you," he said grabbing my ass with one hand and rubbing my slowly protruding belly with the other.

I was currently five months pregnant with our twins, Marisol and Emerald Jr. I couldn't wait to be a mother but I was still somewhat afraid after already losing one child. Emerald prayed over me every night and every morning that he was home. And when he wasn't home, he prayed for me over the phone. It was a powerful thing to have a man that went to God about you. He not only prayed for me, but he prayed for himself, for strength to be the type of man that could love me correctly.

He smiled at me now and kissed my lips.

"I missed you baby," he said. He had just gotten home from a ten-city tour and I couldn't be happier to have him back.

"I missed you too, Em," I said wrapping my arms around his waist.

"First day open for business tomorrow, huh?"

"Yes! I'm so excited!"

"I'm happy for you, Rhyon. You more than deserve this."

"Thank you for making this all possible, Emerald. I wouldn't be here without you."

"Yes you would have. Because you have always been the strong, determined, independent queen I've known and loved all these years. You were destined for greatness baby. I'd go to the ends of the earth to make that happen for you."

"How did I get so lucky?" I asked staring into his beautiful brown eyes.

"I ask myself that every single day," he said flicking my nose.

I rested my head on his chest, listening to the sound of our hearts beating in sync as they always had.

He was mine and I was always his to have.

The End

Made in the USA
Columbia, SC
09 January 2023

75178794R00039